THIS BOOK BELONGS TO

_____

PUPS SAVE A TRAIN

It was a sunny day in Adventure Bay!
Chase and Rubble were busy cleaning up
the sandbox. Rubble even made a
bulldozer out of sand for the kids.

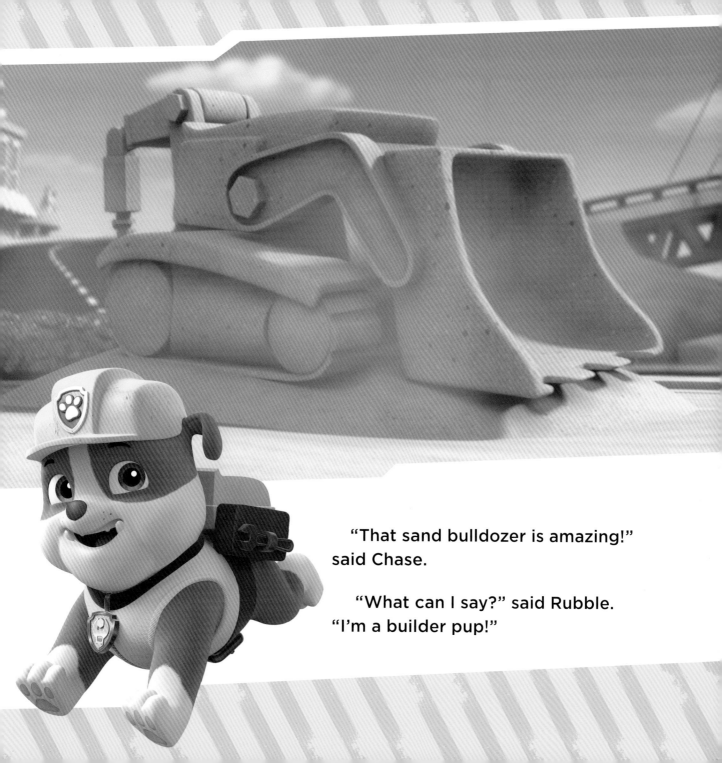

"That sand bulldozer is amazing!"
said Chase.

"What can I say?" said Rubble.
"I'm a builder pup!"

Meanwhile, Katie and her cat, Cali, were on a train. They were returning home after visiting Katie's grandma. Cali reached for a bag of treats.

"Sorry, Cali," Katie said. "Grandma made these treats especially for the PAW Patrol."

Suddenly, the train started shaking and screeched to a halt. There was a rock slide on the tracks!

Katie called Ryder for help.

"The PAW Patrol is on the way," said Ryder. "No job is too big, no pup is too small!"

The pups were playing soccer outside when their pup tags lit up.

"PAW Patrol to the Lookout!" Ryder called.

The pups changed into their uniforms.

"PAW Patrol is ready for action!" said Chase.

"There's been a rockslide on the old trestle bridge,"
Ryder said. "The train is trapped."

"Katie's on that train!" said Skye.

Ryder needed Rubble to scoop up the boulders with his bulldozer.

"Let's dig it!" said Rubble.

Ryder also needed Rocky to haul the boulders away in his recycling truck.

"Green means go!" said Rocky.

PAW PATROL
ARE ON A ROLL!

Ryder, Rubble, and Rocky zoomed across town to the bridge.

When they arrived, Katie and Cali popped their heads out of the train window. They sure were happy to see their friends!

But Cali was still hungry. Outside, the kitty spotted a seagull with some food, and instead of waiting for the PAW Patrol, Cali went out the window to follow the bird!

"We just need to clear the rocks so we can get the train off the bridge," said Ryder.

LET'S DIG IT!

"Rubble on the double!" barked the construction pup. He used his bulldozer to scoop up the boulders and put them in Rocky's truck.

Ryder hurried down the hill. Oh, no! One of the trestles was cracked. Ryder had an idea.

"One of those logs by the road should work great," he said into his helmet mike.

But the hill was too steep for Rocky's truck to make it down with a log.

"We need an extra set of paws," said Ryder.

Ryder called the Lookout.

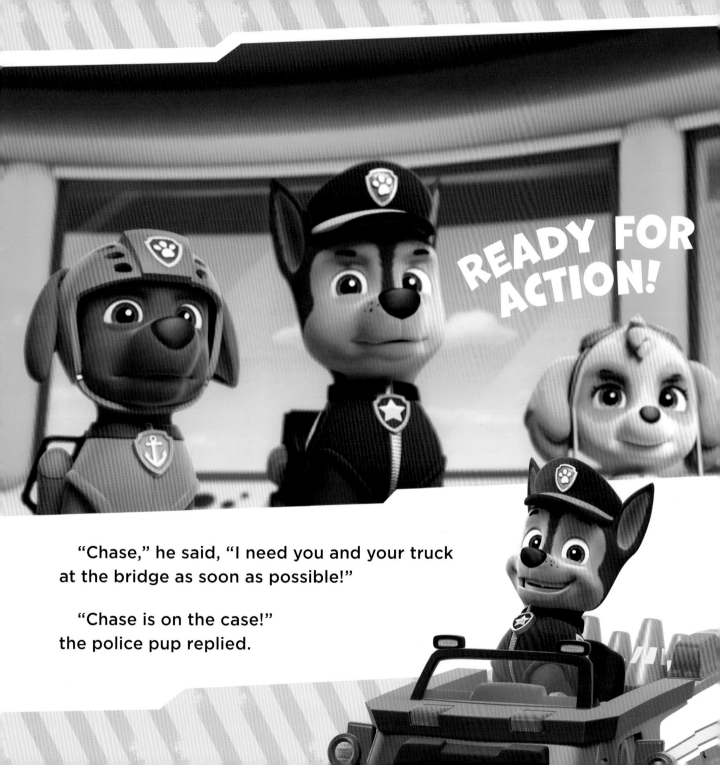

"Chase," he said, "I need you and your truck at the bridge as soon as possible!"

"Chase is on the case!" the police pup replied.

Chase arrived at the scene.

"We need your winch to lower this log to the bridge," said Ryder. "We'll use it to hold up the broken beam."

Chase attached the log to the winch while Rubble used his bulldozer to push the log over the edge of the hill.

Ryder and Rocky put the log in place.

"That'll hold until we get the train off the bridge," he said.

Ryder called Katie. "Tell the engineer that the tracks are all clear," he said.

But Katie was worried. Cali was missing!

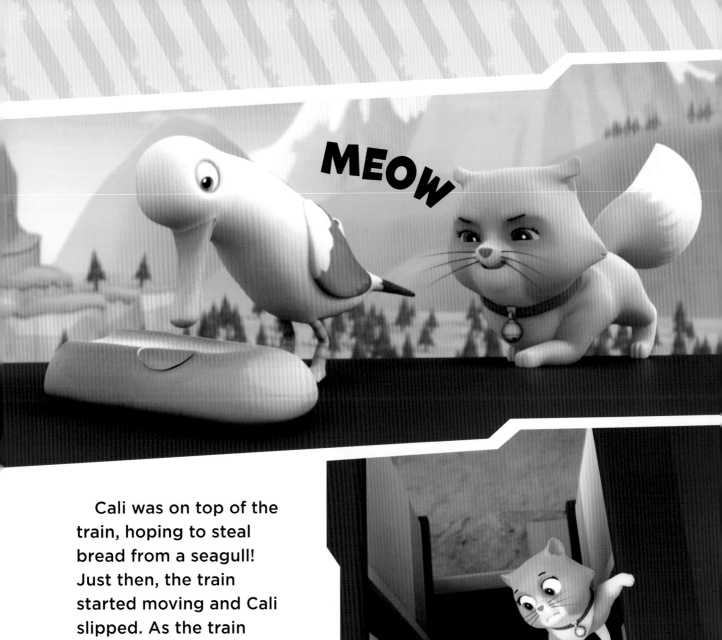

Cali was on top of the train, hoping to steal bread from a seagull! Just then, the train started moving and Cali slipped. As the train rolled along, she hung on with one paw.

It's Chase to the rescue!
He helped Cali up to safety.

Later at the park, Katie thanked the PAW Patrol.

"You guys were awesome," she said reaching into a blue and red bag. "Grandma sent treats!"

She tossed each pup a treat . . . and hungry Cali got one, too!